HALLOWEEN JOKE BOOK

BY DAVID LEWMAN

Simon Spotlight / Nickelodeon

New York London Toronto Sydney Singapore

Based on the TV series *CatDog*® created by Peter Hannan as seen on Nickelodeon®

SIMON SPOTLIGHT

An imprint of Simon & Schuster Children's Publishing Division
1230 Avenue of the Americas, New York, New York 10020

Manufactured in the United States of America

First Edition   2 4 6 8 10 9 7 5 3 1

ISBN 0-689-83387-3

Why did Cat get mad at Dog for carving pumpkins?

He was making faces behind Cat's back.

Which monster loves to play tricks?

Prankenstein.

How did the ghost do
at the scaring
contest?

He won the boo ribbon.

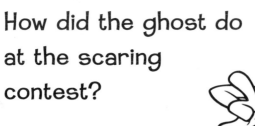

What happens
when a goose
gets scared?

It gets
peoplebumps.

What is every witch's favorite
musical instrument?

The hagpipes.

Where does the Wolfman live?

In a werehouse.

What's the
difference between
a computer and a
vampire?

*One has bytes of memory
and the other has memories of bites.*

How did the night crawler escape
the witch's brew?

He wormed his way out of it.

On Halloween, why did Winslow send the Greasers to CatDog?

He wanted to give CatDog the creeps.

What do vampire chickens say?

"I want to cluck your blood!"

Why did the pumpkin have bad luck?

A black cat crossed its patch.

Where do ghosts surf?

Maliboo!

What do you get when you cross a ghost and a reindeer?

A cariboo.

Was the witches' Halloween show popular?

Yes, it was standing broom only.

What do you call a hot dog on October 31?

A Halloweenie.

Ghost teacher: . . . *and that, students, is how we deal with walls.*

Ghost student: *Could you go through it again?*

Why won't Eddie the Squirrel visit Dog?

He's afraid of the bark.

Eddie the Squirrel: *What do you get when you cross a chicken and an alien?*

Mervis: *An eggstraterrestrial.*

Why did Cliff keep Dog's brother in his sack of treats?

He didn't want to let the Cat out of the bag.

Cat: *Which snake likes to tend sheep?*

Dog: *Little Bo Creep.*

Cliff: **What do witches watch on TV?**

Shriek: *The All Warts Network.*

Cat: **What do you get if you cross a pumpkin and a monster?**

Winslow: *Gourdzilla.*

Cat: **What did Winslow do when the witch turned him into a gorilla?**

Dog: *He went ape.*

Winslow: **What do vampires send to movie stars?**

Dog: *Fang mail.*

Cat: **What do you call a great painting by Frankenstein?**

Dog: **A monsterpiece.**

Cat: **What has orange skin, slimy seeds and wheels?**

Dog: **A skategourd.**

Mr. Sunshine: **What did the ghost say to the passengers on the haunted airplane?**

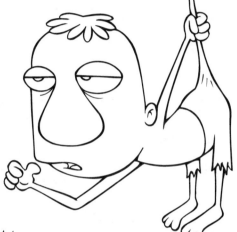

Winslow: *"Have a nice fright!"*

How do ghosts keep in touch?

On their cellular moans.

Cat: **What did the potato do when he saw a ghost?**

Dog: *He jumped out of his skin!*

Did Dracula plan to turn into a bat?

No, he was just winging it.

Cat: **What did the little ghost cry when he wasn't sure who to scare?**

Dog: *"Boo who?"*

Dog: *How did the ghosts build their own haunted house?*

Winslow: *They followed a booprint.*

Mr. Sunshine: *What did the ghost buy for his stereo?*

Cat: *A new set of shriekers.*

Cat: **W**hy did the witch go to the doctor?

Dog: **S**he stubbed her toad.

Dog: **W**hat do witches wear to the beach?

Cat: **S**untan potion.

Cliff: **W**hat did the witch turn **S**ir **L**ancelot into?

Shriek: **A** newt in shining armor.

Mervis: **What do you call a green boat with warts?**

Cat: **A witch craft.**

Which story is about a mad scientist who turns himself into a bee?

Dr. Jekyll and Mr. Hive.

What do you call a ghost who haunts classrooms?

School spirit.

What is every ghoul's favorite ride?

The roller ghoster.

What is every ghost's favorite instrument?

The spookulele.

What was wrong with the ghost's car?

It needed new spook plugs.

What's big and gray and wears a mask?

The Elephantom of the Opera.

What did the turkey go as on Halloween?

A gobblin'.

What kind of ghosts haunt the beach?

Sea ghouls.

What kind of ghosts play the most pranks?

April ghouls.

What's big and green and goes "oink oink?"

Frankenswine.

Why did the mummy excuse himself?

He had to go to the rest tomb.

Dog: **Are witches good gardeners?**

Cat: **Yes, they all have green thumbs.**

If Cat and Dog were mummies, where would they live?

In a pair-amid.

Cat: **Knock, knock.**
Dog: **Who's there?**
Cat: **Spear.**
Dog: **Spear who?**

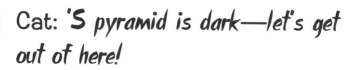

Cat: **'S** pyramid is dark—let's get out of here!

Where do cat mummies
come from?

Purr-amids.

If Winslow was a mummy, where
would he live?

In a sneer-amid.

Who's the best mummy wrapper in Egypt?

The **Wizard** *of* **Gauze***.*

Why did the musician mummy leave the pyramid?

To join a rock bandage.

Why did the skeleton dye eggs?

*He wanted to be the **Easter** Boney.*

What did he put the eggs in?

*His **Easter** casket.*

Where do skeletons buy their clothes?

At back-to-skull sales.

Where do zombies go before junior high school?

Grave school.

What basketball position did the zombie play?

Dead center.

What did he keep getting called for?

Ghoultending.

Who won the race between the skeleton and the zombie?

It was a dead heat.

What do mommy zombies read to their children?

Ghouldilocks and the Three Scares.

Why don't zombies drive?

They always come to a dead end.

What do you get when you cross a ghoul and a dog?

A zombeagle.

What do you get when you cross a ghoul and a cow?

Zombeef.

How do you spot the best vampires?

They have the highest batting averages.

What would Cat and Dog be if they were like Dracula?

A vampair.

What would Dog be if he were a vampire?

A bloodhound.

How do you spot a vampire?

You can tell right off the bat.

Why wouldn't Dog make a scary vampire?

His bark is worse than his bite.

What do vampires drive?

Bloodmobiles.

What are vampires' pajamas made out of?

100 percent coffin.

Why do vampires like fishing?

They get lots of bites.

Which vampire wears really boring clothes?

Count Drabula.

Are vampires crazy?

No, but at night they get a little batty.

What do you get when you cross a snowman and a vampire?

Frostbite.

What do you call a man who turns into a sheep every full moon?

A werewool.

What's a werewolf's motto?

"Eat, drink, and be hairy."

Where do great werewolves end up?

In the Howl of Fame.

Why did CatDog go
in the haunted
house?

They just wanted to let off a little
scream.

What did the mother ghost say
to the kid ghost?

"Don't boo with your mouth full!"

What do you get when you cross a wild dog and a pumpkin?

A jackal-lantern.

What does Cat say on Halloween?

"Trick or trout!"

Dog: **Why are you so suspicious of pumpkins?**

Cat: *Because they're seedy characters.*

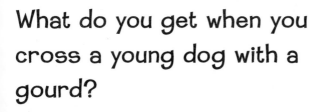

What do you get when you cross a young dog with a gourd?

A pupkin.

What does Dog
say on
Halloween?

"Trick or meat!"

What do you call an overweight
jack-o-lantern?

A plumpkin.

Why do spiders like ducks?

Because of their webbed feet.

What do witches serve on Halloween?

Apple spider.

Where did the spider catch an ear of corn?

In a cobweb.

What kind of witch always brightens things up?

A light switch.

Why wouldn't the witch's broom fly?

It was too sweepy.

What do you call Dog's brother when he dives for apples?

Bob Cat.

Why was CatDog's house haunted by a new ghost every four weeks?

Dog joined the Spook-of-the-Month Club.

What do you call spuds in Halloween costumes?

Masked potatoes.

Dog: *Knock, knock.*
Cat: *Who's there?*
Dog: *Ogre.*
Cat: *Ogre who?*

Dog: *Oh, grrrr—the Greasers are here.*

Why do ghosts make
bad audiences?

All they do is boo!